HEARTSTOPPER
VOLUME 2

Heartstopper: Volume 2 was originally published in England
by Hachette Children's Group in 2019.

Library of Congress Control Number: 2019950316

ISBN 978-1-338-61749-8 (hardcover)
ISBN 978-1-338-61747-4 (paperback)

10 9 8 7 6 5 4 3 2 1   20 21 22 23 24

Printed in China 167
This edition first printing, November 2020

ALICE OSEMAN
HEARTSTOPPER
VOLUME 2
graphix
An Imprint of
SCHOLASTIC

4/17
I've. Destroyed. Everything.
Me and Nick have been friends for, what, four months now? It sounds like no time at all but it feels like FOREVER. He's my best friend in the whole world. I don't
HI
HI
know how that happened. First we were just two guys who sat next to each other in class. Then he asked me to join rugby - OBVIOUSLY I said yes, just so
That was...okay?
Yep! Perfect pass!
I could hang out with him more. Then we were going to each other's houses. Telling each other everything.

But then I had to go and kiss him.
stupid stupid STUPID
Of course he rejected me.
of course.
God, that look in his eyes when he walked away...
I guess that's what happens when you fall for a straight boy.

3. KISS

LATER THAT NIGHT...

Hi, Dad... could you come and pick me up early?
SIGH Fine. Did something happen?
No...
I just didn't have anyone to hang out with.
I thought your friend Nick was gonna be there?
He stayed with his Year 11 friends.

ngh...
sniff
SQUEEZE

...Nick? Are you even listening to me?
I have to go
What the fuck!!
EMPTY
Charlie??

SIT UP

fvck

TAP
TAP
TAP
2:17
Charlie
ok! my dad's dropping me off at about 7:30pm so you'll probably get there before me! see you there
cool!! see you there!!
Hey Charlie I'm so so sorry for running off and leaving you it wasn't your fault I was just
2:17
Charlie
ok! my dad's dropping me off at about 7:30pm so you'll probably get there before me! see you there
cool!! see you there!!
Charlie I'm so so sorry I don't know what's wrong with me, I'm just so confused right now but

DELETE
MI

THROW

fuck

THE NEXT MORNING
<2 HOURS OF SLEEP
NO NEW MESSAGES
10:34
Sunday, April 18
GAY

Sigh
...are you okay?
Yeah
...
SHREDD
CORN
sip

BRUSH
BRUSH

♡

Would you kiss me?

DING DONG
CHARLIE can you get the door, please? It's probably the postman
mum
FINE! one sec

FSSSSSHHHHH
...hi
N-Nick
東京都

Sorry for not texting you, I just- I just wanted to talk in person
O-okay

...

GRAB
just- just
come in
you're
getting
soaked
PULL

erm...
s-so...
I just-
CHARLIE'S MUM
Nick?
I didn't know you were coming over?
um-er-yes-
HE'S JUST PICKING UP A JUMPER HE LEFT HERE LAST WEEK
TOKYO
TOKYO

You could have at least changed out of your PJs, Charlie!
Oh... yeah
Don't forget we're going to Grandma's later
Let's go upstairs
Okay
flatten

deep breath
SHUT
BRIDESHEAD REVISITED

So... did you forget a coat??
O-oh... yeah
I didn't check the weather before I left...
TOKYO
東京都
OK
COOL

er, so -
WAIT
Can I speak first?
I'm just
so sorry

WAIT
WHAT
I'm so sorry, it was- I didn't think properly about what I was doing and it was a stupid thing to do and-
a-and I don't want you to feel awkward about it because it was all my fault
Charlie, hang on-

I SHOULDN'T HAVE KISSED YOU
It was so rude and I bet you just felt pressured to do it because I asked
and I know you probably don't want to talk to me **ever again**
NDRY
Um... Charlie-

Which is FAIR ENOUGH
I'd completely understand
LAUNDRY
Charlie...

but I had to at least say sorry
STEP
a-and see if maybe-
Charlie-
-there's a chance we could still be friends

I DON'T WANT TO LOSE YOU BECAUSE I DID SOMETHING STUPID
Charlie
You're p-probably the best friend
Charlie
I've
e-ever
had

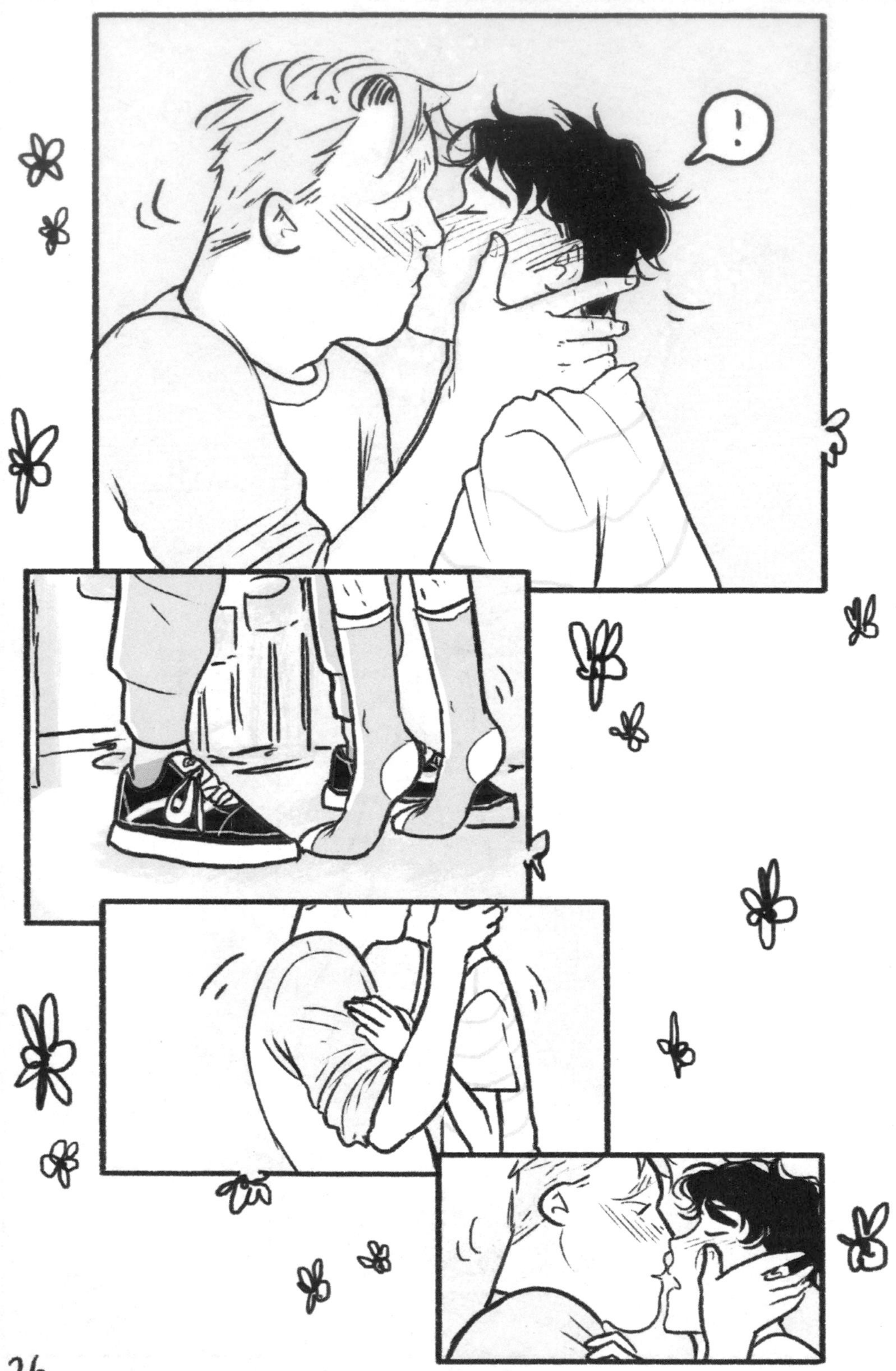

PANT
PANT
PANT
...♡
exhale

MUSE
...
u-um...
you...
you've been sending me a lot of mixed signals

...
HA
HA
HA
HA
HA
...
... Jesus Christ

God...
I'm so sorry ...
PAT
PAT

I'm just...
SO SORRY
I ran away
I was just FREAKING OUT
like honestly I am having a proper full-on GAY CRISIS
...

It's not that I didn't want to...

you know...
kiss you

I was just so confused...
MUSIC
The Strokes
I've just been so, so confused...

A-and I didn't expect that to happen yesterday
It's not like I didn't WANT to but I hadn't really psyched myself up and then bloody Sai turns up and I wanted to stay with you, but... b-but...

but I didn't want other people to- to see us doing that
I mean, I'm not ashamed, I'm just... it was just...
I j-just need some time to figure this out

I just need a bit more time

I'm sorry
It's okay
MUSIC
It's okay

PLIP

Sniff

Wait, why are you crying?

sniff I just... seeing you sad makes me sad

Pfft

Ha ha ha!

Now I've messed up both times we've kissed
Why can't we just kiss and be happy?

You haven't messed it up
And I'm really happy
BRUSH
so am I

NUZZLE
Do you want a cup of tea?
Yes please
E RESIS
SATURN

BOOP
HA
HA
PFFT
BOOP
HA
HA
HA
HA
SIP

PATTER
Are you sure your family won't... erm... want to use this room?
PATTER
PATTER
PATTER
Nah, no one really sits in the conservatory in the mornings
Okay

BLOW
SIP
How did you realize you're gay?

oh
er
I guess I've always been sort of aware of it...
even when I was really young...

From my fictional crushes
to my real ones
I suppose I didn't understand it at the time, but...
It's always been boys

I'm guessing you didn't feel the same when you were little
Well... no
HA
HA
HA
Do your parents know?
SIP
Yeah. And my brother and sister. They're all really chill about it.
SIP

I... don't know what I am...
I've liked girls before ...
but now...
I like you

you like me?
Was that not obvious?
I'm an idiot

I thought... I just really liked you as a friend... a best friend... because, like, I want to hang out with you all the time and I just love everything about you...

but I kept wanting to... I don't know... hug you and hold your hand

and then yesterday, when you suggested it, I- I really wanted to kiss you

I SHOULDN'T HAVE RUN AWAY FROM YOU I'M SO SORRY
NO NO I SHOULD HAVE JUST TOLD YOU I LIKE YOU INSTEAD OF JUST KISSING YOU
You like me, too??
??yes? obviously?
...
HA HA HA
PFFT HA HA HA
Why are we like this??

FSSSSH
I would have said something sooner, but I convinced myself you were straight.
I don't know what I am now

Well...
you could
be
bisexual?
o-or
something
else! There
are lots
of sexualities
other than
gay and
straight!
bisexual...

ANYWAY you don't have to work it out, like, immediately
I didn't just wake up one day like-
OH LOOK, guess I'm gay now!
HAHA!

Well...
Sorry for being all confused
Now look who's saying sorry too much!
Hey!!
HA HA HA
SHOVE

FSSSSH
What do I do now?
You don't have to do anything
But I want to

FSSSSH
FSSSSH

Ha ha I'm so bad at this
You're not ♡

OLIVER SPRING
NICK'S HERE?!?
Yeah, they're in the conservatory
OPEN

...
NICK!!
!!!
H-Hey, Olly! You okay?
Yep! ♡

Charlie?
Yes?
Were you and Nick KISSING?
er... no, we were just... hugging
HA HA HA but I saw your lips touching!

SHRUG
You've got to keep it a secret, okay? It can be a secret between us three!
Okay
And Mum said we're leaving to go to Grandma's in five minutes

So... would it be okay if we kept us a secret? Just for a little while

I'm sorry, I just don't think I'm ready to come out as anything yet-
GRAB
It's fine, Nick. I'm just glad we're okay now.

Although I wish I didn't look like an absolute MESS
You don't ...
You look... really cute

You always...
You always look really cute
HA HA HA

Come on, Charlie! We're leaving soon!
Oh yeah, you should borrow this
haha thanks!
...
I'll text you later!!
Okay!!

PATTER

PATTER

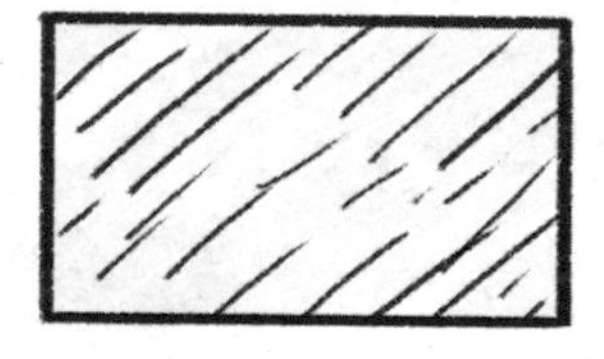

NICK!
?

D-Did I forget something?
PATTER
PATTER

GLANCE
GLANCE

OKAY BYE!

HA
HA
HA!
TOKYO

TAP
TAP
TAP
LATER...
9:07
NICK
You sure it's okay to keep it a secret at school???
OF COURSE seriously I know what it's like to have something spread around school before you're ready
Shit yeah ☹
i promise i don't mind!!

i promise i don't mind!!
PING
Why are you so great ♡

PING
Why are you so great ♡♡
the nicer i am to you, the more chances i will get to hang out with your dog
HA HA
SNAP
SEND

TAP
TA P
TAP
TAP
alksjdfhajhdsf
i just died
you can't just send me that without warning!!!!!
HA
HA
HA

yeah you know i'm only getting with you so i can see Nellie right
I KNEW IT
Who are you texting?
NO ONE

PLACE
CLICK
Being bisexual means you're attracted to more than one gender, so not JUST girls or not JUST guys-
What is bisexuality?

MONDAY
hi
hi

ha ha!
?
SQUEEZE
?
There's a bug in your hair
Well... see you tomorrow
Y-yeah! See you tomorrow

TUESDAY

$a^2 + b^2 = c^2$
hyp
θ
adj
$A = \pi r^2$
r
ALED↓
↓TAO
...
It's worse than I thought. He still hasn't given up on Nick Nelson.

WEDNESDAY
oh no

Oh-
whoops-
Holy shit, Charlie!
okay
Christ, sorry, Charlie, I forgot how light you are-
CHARLIE!!
are you okay??
PULL
um y-yeah I think so

STEP
ah
You're hurt!!
n-no I'm f-fine

?
Miss, I'm just getting Charlie an ice pack!
...
...
...
LIMP

...that's a bit g-
OKAY BACK TO THE GAME, LADS
CHRISTIAN
SAI

Okay, this'll be cold
CHANGING ROOM
I mean.. I kind of expected that

You didn't have to do this
Seriously...
I don't mind if you wanna be a bit more distant at school-
Hey!

I promise I'm not doing anything I don't want to do
Just because I want to keep us a secret doesn't mean we have to start ignoring each other
Also...
we're not really acting any different to before we kissed
apart from doing stuff like this
I... I guess so

Uh... I thought...
...we were gonna try not to kiss at school...
Hmm...
just one more kiss then...

THURSDAY
I looked up what bisexual means

I've been reading about it all week and...
...I think that might be me
but I'm still not sure

That's okay! You don't have to be sure! You don't even have to think about it!
Haha... It's pretty much all I've been thinking about lately
Well...
let me distract you then...

RUSTLE
ROLL

?
?
Sorry

Don't be sorry!!
I feel bad...
Nick. I understand. I promise.

Can I have an extra kiss when we get back to your house?
y-yeah!!
boof?

FRIDAY
So... it's kind of my birthday next Tuesday
me and my friends are going bowling tomorrow
and... um... I was gonna ask if you wanted to come but I know you don't really know my friends so you don't have to-

YES!
!
Nick and Charlie! Keep it down, please!
Thanks for giving me barely any time to get you a present!
NUDGE
You don't have to get me a present...

Yeah, Charlie's dad's dropping me home
Okay! Have fun!
BOWLING

SHUT
PUSH
Hey!
15
RECEPTION

Happy birthday!
Haha! It's not my birthday till Tuesday!
!! I said you didn't have to get me anything!!
And I ignored you

Am I the first person here??
Haha no, you're actually the last
Oh
We're over there! Lane seven.
7

!
That's Tao. Sorry in advance if he says anything rude to you. That's just the way he is.
That's Aled. He's really shy but I promise he's really nice.
Hey, isn't that-
Her name's Elle now! She moved to the all-girls school last year after she came out as trans.

I think she and Tao kind of like each other, but...
They haven't said anything about it to anyone...
Kind of like us, then? ♡
Um... I guess so!
15
Hey everyone, so...
7
8

This is Nick
Hi!
What name d'you want me to put on the board?
Haha just Nick is fine!
Hey, Elle! How's Higgs school?
Mostly the same as Truham. But cleaner.
USED TO HAVE GEOGRAPHY CLASS TOGETHER

BIRTHDAY BOY	6	2	8
ALED :)	3	2	5
ELLE SMELLS	X		
BEANIE (TAO)	3	0	3
NICK	8	/	

STRIKE!

Looks like Nick won the first game!!
YES!!!...
GAME 1 WINNER
NICK!
Noooo! I was so close!
CLAP CLAP
You totally cheated
Oh yeah? How?

You... You have strong rugby arms!!
Oh do I now ...
I thought you liked my arms
Pfft shut up!!

HA HA HA

...
Everyone ready for game 2?
I'm just gonna go pee!
Okay!
...
!
!

I'm gonna go talk to him
Huh? About what?
GAME 2
START
MGP
You know
?
GAME 2
START
MGP
I won't be long
NO, Tao- don't-
GAME 2
START
MGP
FSSHHH

Charlie.
?
Oh hey, Tao!

Charlie, look, I'm saying this to you as a friend-

You need to STOP this thing with Nick Nelson

Hmm I think I'm gonna go get more chips

Gotta get energized for game 2?
I need to defend my title
Bar

He's clearly straight and he's leading you on!!
?

Wh-what
He's flirting with you for a laugh!!

That's... that's not true
Come ON. Even I can tell he's flirting with you
And you think he's straight just because he doesn't LOOK gay??
WELL? Isn't he straight?
...
...
SEE! You KNOW he's just an attention seeker like Harry and the rest of his mates!

He's not like that
He's ...
He's my ...

He's my...
Would it be okay if we kept us a secret?
He's my friend

But you clearly like him
So what?
So you're never gonna get over it until you cut him out of your life!
Well, I'm not going to.
Why do you keep nagging at me about this? Nick is one of my best friends now
And that's NOT GONNA CHANGE!

I'm- I'm just worried-
Worried about WHAT?
I'm worried that... one day he'll find out you like him and... I don't know... do something bad.
Like, a lot of his Year 11 friends like Harry are kinda judgmental and exactly the sort of people who bullied you last year.
I was the only one on your side back then, and... I'm so scared that'll happen to you again
...

We weren't close with Aled and Elle back then. They don't know what it was like.
You used to be terrified to come to school.
And I couldn't do anything to help.

sigh why didn't you just say that
I PROMISE Nick's not like that. He's different. Trust me.
You've just got to get to know him!

Okay, fine.
But if he even HINTS that he might be a dick–
Yeah yeah yeah, you'll report him to our head of house, I know.

!
UGH just go. I'll meet you back at our lane.

You getting more food?
Yep!
haha
you're gonna need it if you wanna beat Elle again-
huh?

h-hey
Wh-what's this for?
I'll tell you later

...
okay
um... have you two been served?
YESSS!

GAME 2 WINNER
ELLE SMELLS!
I WIN
ughhh why do I always lose
CLAP CLAP
It's because you have such adorably short arms, Tiny Tao
SHUT UP!!
and don't call me that
Just stating the facts, Tiny. No need to blush!
go away

Bye!

see you on Monday!

Thanks for coming, Aled :)

Thanks for inviting me!

Oh, and... Nick's really nice. I'm glad you're... I'm glad you two are... um...

I'm glad he's here!

Bye!

b-bye?

What'd I miss?
WENT TO THE BATHROOM
Haha, everyone had to go
My dad won't be here for another ten minutes so shall we go sit?
FOLD
Ok ♡
By the way... Tao and Elle really do like each other, don't they?
BAR
Haha yep. Neither of them will admit it, though.
15

So...
you gonna open my present?
Oh!! As long as you don't mind??
I kinda wanna see your reaction, haha...

HAPPY BIRTHDAY!
RIP
Snow Day

You decorated this yourself?
Yeah... sorry I didn't have time to buy you anything! That was one of my favorite days ever, so...
I wanna kiss you so bad right now

Menu
Menu
Menu
Okay

Are you sure??
Yeah

Ha ha

NUZZLE
Hey...
I... overheard you and Tao in the bathroom earlier
Oh. Oh no.
You don't believe what he said, do you? I'm not- I'm not just doing this for a laugh or attention-
No! Of course not!

Yeah... I don't know why I thought you'd believe that
Tao can be very forceful about his opinions
I'm so scared I'm just...
doing to you what Ben did to you-

NO.
You're NOTHING like him.
Okay
I wish being out wasn't so terrifying to me.

yeah, I've been there.
I... remember when you used to get bullied.
I wish I'd... helped you, or... done something, I don't know.
?
But you didn't even know me then!

I wish I had known you
I wish I'd known then what I know now

Maybe then I would have helped...
Hey!
POKE
no being sad on my birthday

I thought it wasn't your birthday until Tuesday!
POKE
Ahh!
Isn't that what you said?
Ha ha ha!
Nick!!

♫
Ah-that's my phone
hi, Dad!
Okay, we'll be out in a sec

MAY
(TWO AND A HALF WEEKS LATER)
Hurry up, Nick, you'll be late for fourth period!
Sorry, sir!
D92
SCRIBBLE
HIGH ACHIEVERS
YEAR 10
George Henderson
Aled Last
Ishmael Leftley
Charles Spring

Surds Homework - Due May 12th
Nick Nelso
1. √12
= √4×3
= √4 × √3
= 2 × √3 = 2√3
2. √12 + √27
= 2√3 + (√9 × √3)
= 2√3 + (3 × √3)
= 2√3 + 3√3
= 5√3
3. 8√6 / 2√3
MATH
SCHOOL HALL
SCIENCE
BUMP!
Oh hey!
Hey!!

Spring Concert
Truham Grammar School for Boys and Harvey Greene Grammar School for Girls
I thought you had Spanish right now?
Yeah, I was supposed to, but...
Our school orchestra is doing a joint concert thing with the girls' school and they needed me to play drums for the rehearsal
Oooh that's cool!
What are you doing? Did you forget to do your math homework again?
Well... I was gonna do it last night, but...

er... you came over and...

...yeah.

Oh.

ha ha!

I'm stuck on a question anyway
Oh! You've just got to deal with each term individually-
How are you better at math than I am?! You're in the year below me!
Hahaha!

Wow.
3.
$\frac{8\sqrt{6}}{2\sqrt{3}}$
$\frac{8}{2} = 4$
$\frac{\sqrt{6}}{\sqrt{3}} = \sqrt{\frac{6}{3}} = \sqrt{2}$
$= 4\sqrt{2}$
Guess I'm just really smart
You are!
Charlie! We need you on drums!
See you later!

CHARLIE!!
Yeah I'm here!

Hey, Nick?

?

Tara!! You're in Higgs School orchestra?
Yep! I'm not that good but we get to play film music so it's pretty fun

You and Charlie Spring still getting along well, then?
We need a simple 4/4 rock beat, okay?
Okay

Oh-
y-yeah,
yeah
...
I'm
gay
actually...
well...
Nick
Nelson
11H

We're...
er...

We're sort of going out

You are?!
I-I mean, we haven't, um, made it official, but... yeah
Uh- please don't tell anyone, though!!
Don't worry, I won't!
You guys keeping it on the down low?
yeah...

Haha...
You're the first person I've told
Does it feel good to have told someone?
LEAN
...yeah
It really does

I remember when me and my girlfriend first told our friends
?
some of them were surprised but a couple of them were like
SNEAK
"haha, we've known for ages"
I guess we weren't that good at being low-key

PARP
DARCY!!
heh heh heh
Got you ♥
Oh my GOD, I hate you

Sooooo...
this is Nick?
...hi?
This is Darcy Olsson. My girlfriend.
!
H G
G S

he... knows??
er... well...
I- I have a ...
I'm going out with Charlie Spring
!

WHAT!!
we've found another one
SSH you can't tell anyone!!
She won't tell anyone
O...kay-
Hey, Nick!!

Oi oi!!
A girl on each arm!
Get in there, my son!
HA HA HA!
... why are straight people like this

So, Nick... you're not out to anyone?
er... I guess not
apart from Charlie and you two
Do you want to be?
...
I feel like... I don't really understand myself enough yet. Like, I'm not even 100% sure what I identify as.

That's okay! Tara didn't know she was a lesbian until we'd kissed like 6 times
Hey...
Nick... don't feel like you need to come out to anyone until you feel ready.
Rumors spread so fast around our schools...
That can be really hard to deal with if you barely know who you are.

That's true...
TARA! DARCY! We're running from the top!
We'd better go
We'll see you again soon, okay? Message us!
Yeah, we need to go on a double date or something!
PAT PAT

Spring Concert
Truham Grammar School for Boys and Harvey Greene Grammar School for Girls
Bye!
Spring Concert
Truham Grammar School for Boys and Harvey Greene Grammar School for Girls
...
I AM SUPER LATE FOR MATH

PRESENT TENSE
AR regular verbs
Take -AR off and add:
(Yo) O
(Tú) AS
(El/Ella/Usted) A
(Nosotros/Nosotras) AMOS
(Vosotros/Vosotras) ÁIS
(Ellos/Ellas) AN
ER regular verbs
2:31
Saturday May 15
BEST COAST
Boyfriend - Best Coast

?
Charlie Spring 10H Spanish
You're staring
You're cute

DO YOUR REVISION!!
THROW
Ha ha ha!!
Hey... so...

You know I saw Tara at the rehearsal the other day?
Oh... yeah?
Did you know she's a lesbian?
WHAT
Haha, she's got a girlfriend, too!

Oh my god...
I was jealous of her for ages because I thought you and her might... you know... get together or something
Okay, that's REALLY cute
Shut up!! I'm so embarrassed!!

Anyway, I told her-
I told her we're together
Wh- what
I told her we're going out

Was... was that okay?
I felt bad because I didn't ask you first-
OH MY GOD!!
THAT'S AMAZING!!

Oh!! My!! God!!
Ha ha ha!!
You're amazing

I take it that means you don't mind I told her?
You told someone!!
You came out to someone!!
I did!!
...

going out with you is like a dream
MATHS

AH- sorry, was that- uh- was that too much-
NO NO, you just- you surprised me!!
Haha okay!!
!!

...
Tori... I didn't hear you get home

What's up?
I got you those pens you wanted
Oh. Thanks.

...
What??

glance

well done

...

SHUT
okay, she's gone, haha!
Nick?
Hey... it's okay. She'd never tell anyone without asking me first.
Sorry... I guess people knowing about us still makes me panic

Nick... you don't need to feel bad about feeling like that. I don't expect you to be okay with coming out to everyone at once!
That's true...
Haha your hair!
Pfft I need a haircut
kiss

So are you sure you want me to come with you next Saturday?
Yeah!!
You invited me out with your friends so you should come out with mine!
I feel like your friends don't like me though...
Hey no no no!!

That's just Harry. Who is a dickhead. And isn't even gonna be there.
Haha okay
See you on Monday?
Yeah
glance

Text me later!
I will!
APPEAR
Hey, Charles
Jesus, how do you just appear out of nowhere?
Older sister magic

SIP
So you're going out with him?
...yeah
You can't tell anyone, okay? Nick's... Nick's working things out. He's not even out to his mum-
Come on, I'm not an idiot. Your secret's safe with me.

I'm happy for you.
You've liked him for ages.
Shut up
By the way... are you sure you want to hang out with his friends?

I've seen them at parties. They're not... They're kind of...
They're not like your friends.
...
I'll be fine.
SIP

THE NEXT SATURDAY...
cinema
CAR PA
Pick up at 10pm, okay?
Yep

... what?
If any of these boys says anything, does anything nasty, you just call me, okay?
...
Nick's gonna be there, I'll be fine!

Hey ♡
Hey ♡

Your hair!!
I know, it's so short. Is it bad?
Yep. It's terrible.
Oh REALLY...
Yeah right, you liiiiike it-
Shuuuut up!!

Hey... you look nervous
Ah-er- well, your friends...
You find them intimidating?
ar. cinema . bar . c
Well... yeah...

I don't know... They probably all just think I'm this... gay nerd...
Well, you are kind of a gay nerd
Shut up, rugby lad!!
Ha ha ha!
PUSH
Don't worry, I'll look after you!
Okay ♡

And it's not like Harry's gonna-
SCREENS 1-8
TICK
Be... here...

He did bring him
Charlie...
...
I'm not gonna let someone like him intimidate me
Hey, guys...
1
2

You all know Charlie, right?
hi!
...
CHRISTIAN
SAI
Hi, Charlie!
Hey, Charlie, you all right, mate?
only

...
ha
ha
ha
ha
ha
Sat May
7:45
Screen 4
Row: G Seat: 10
Ah, I forgot to ask!
Are you okay with horror movies?
Yeah, I love horror!
RIP
cinema

Well, I get really scared, so, sorry if I scream really loud in your ear
NUDGE
Well, I'll be next to you if you need to hold my hand
Hey, let's get popcorn!
PULL

Oh... I'm... not very hungry, to be honest
You get some, though
brush
Hey...

Seriously, Char,
are you okay?
I honestly had no idea he'd be here
I wouldn't have suggested we come if I'd known
"Char"?

Oh... er, wow, th-that just slipped out-
Oh my GOD, say it again!!
NO!!
Go onnnnn
No!!!
I like it. It's cute.
Now I'm never calling you it again

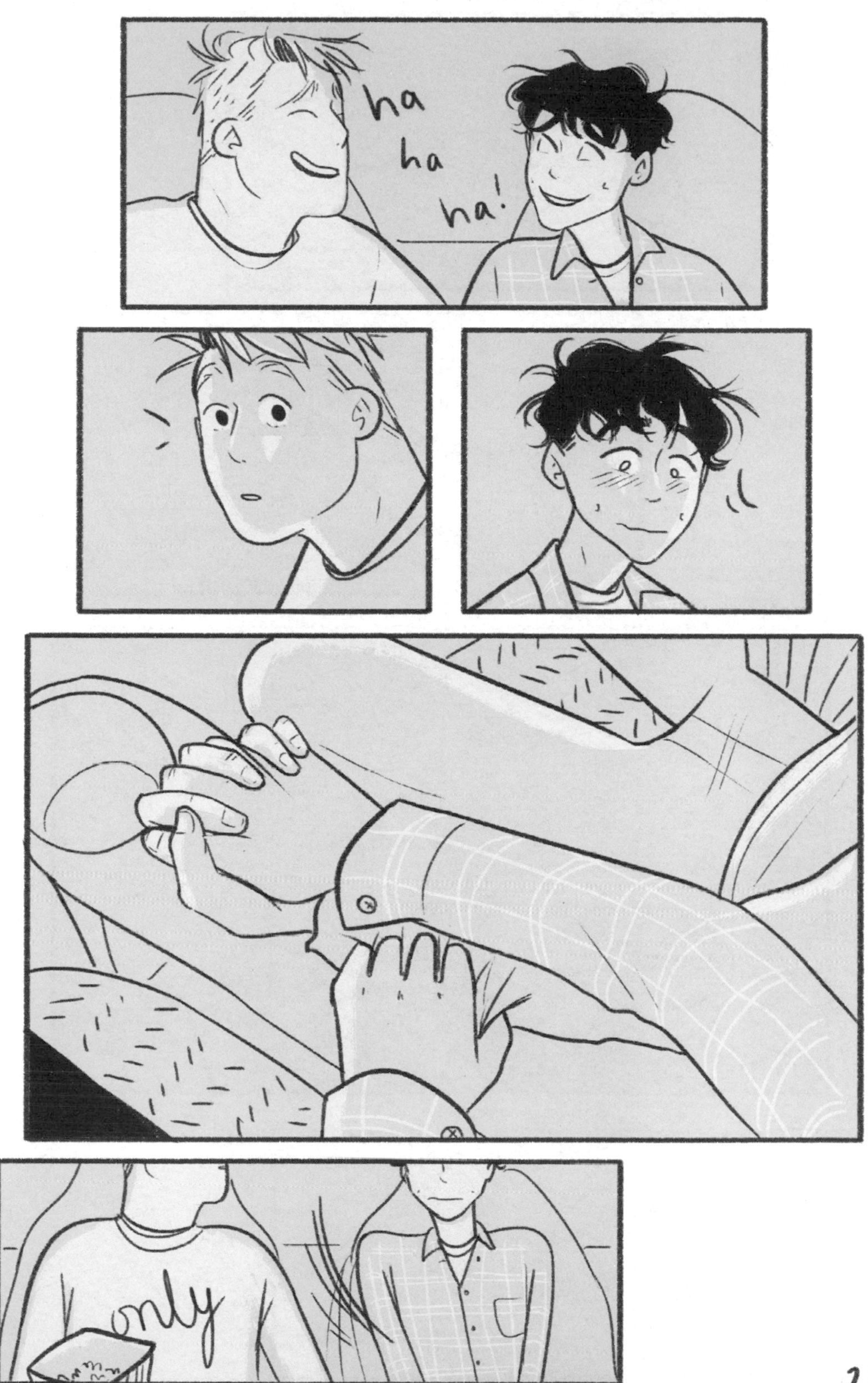
ha
ha
ha!
only

sorry
...
...

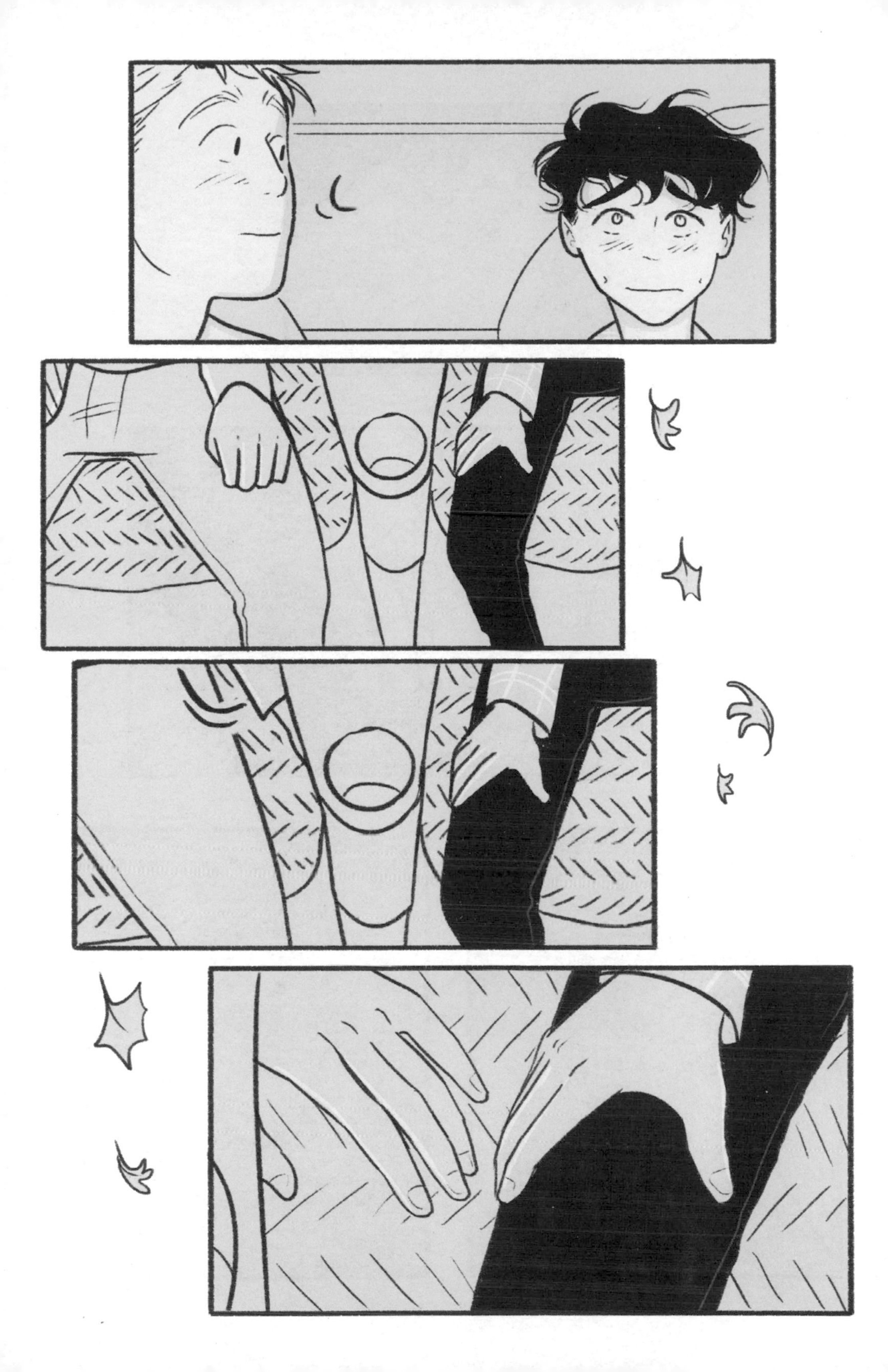

You're a dork
That was soooo scary
For you maybe
Uh, you SO jumped at all the jump scares
I did NOT!

!
SO! Charlie Spring!
What's it like being GAY?
It's... fine??
PUSH

You don't seem that gay, to be honest
I mean, you SOUND sort of gay, but that's it!
Do you like musicals?
HARRY, can you just fuck off, please?
only

What sort of guys do you like, then?
I don't know.
What about... Zayn Malik?! He's pretty sexy!
I guess.
Harry, for fuck's sake-
What about Nick? You think he's hot?
That's-

Not really my type.
...
Naaah, you SO have a crush on him!
No.
You dooo

You'd sooooo jump on that DICK-
GRAB
PUSH
only

Come on, let's go
Saturday, May 22
Dad
I'm here
Ah, my dad's here, I have to go...
Charlie ...

Hey, hey, wait-
huh?
God, I'm so sorry-
No, Harry was being an absolute twat and the others were being really unfriendly to you! We- we should have just left-
I- It's fine-

It's fine, Nick, it's honestly fine, I'm used to it by now!
...
Hey, no.
It's not fine.
You're always covering for me. Because you're the kindest, most thoughtful and sweet and amazing person in the whole world.
But-

I don't want you to have to do that anymore.
Nick...
BEEP!!

Ah... I really need to go
er- message me later?
Yeah!

Go on, then.
What's your problem with Charlie?
Well he doesn't exactly fit in with us, does he?
Yeah, you can't just bring some gay kid and expect us to automatically like him.
So this is a problem with him being gay.
Come on, Nick, none of us are homophobic here.

You can shut the fuck up.
You made him SO uncomfortable with all your gay questions.
Oh wow, someone needs to learn how to take a joke!
You WEREN'T joking though, were you.
You just saw the perfect opportunity to make someone feel like shit.
As usual.

I'm sure he can deal with it. He's probably used to it by now.
I'm used to it by now..
SHOVE
Aw, you're getting so ANGRY!

SHOVE
You just can't help wanting to protect him, can you!
Because he's a pathetic-
little-

fag
GRAB
PUNCH

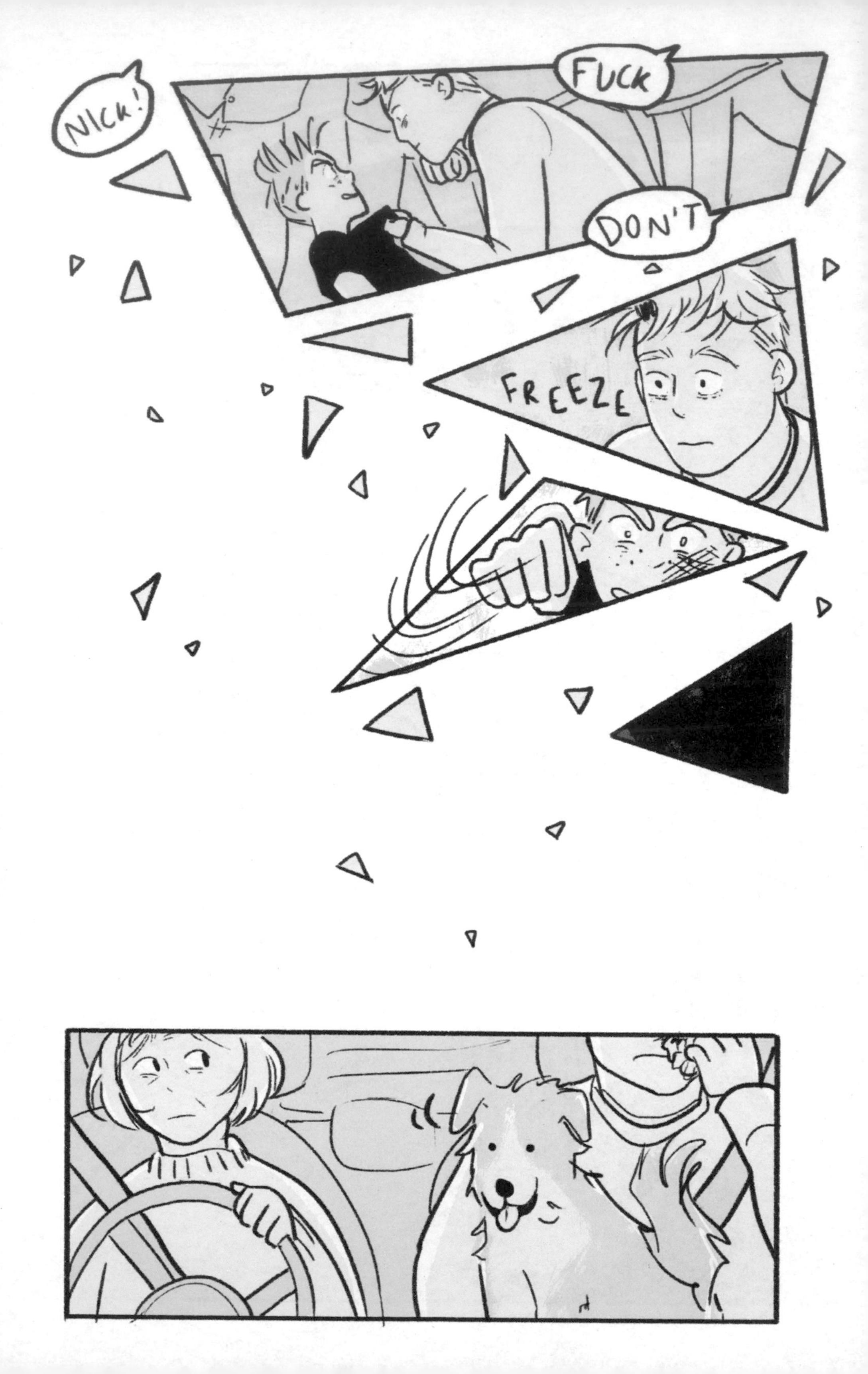
NICK!
FUCK
DON'T
FREEZE

You gonna tell me what happened?
There's not really anything to tell.
Nicky. Come on, baby.
Harry was saying really nasty stuff about-
-about Charlie

He's been really gross and mean about Charlie for ages and I just...
I just finally lost it.
I'm so angry at myself for not seeing how horrible all my friends are until now...
Oh, baby... you know fighting's not the answer
I know, but he was being really shitty
Nicholas
Sorry

Charlie's a really special friend, isn't he
...
He's-

SQUEEEZE

yeah

yeah he is

BUZZ
11:46
Saturday, May 22
Nick
Hey you awake?

TAP
TAP
Always haha
I'm so sorry about tonight, all my friends are ASSHOLES
No I'm sorry I shouldn't have agreed to come!!
HEY
NO
YOU'RE NOT ALLOWED TO SAY THE S WORD
TAP
TAP
TAP

TAP
TAP
TAP
I don't want to be friends with those guys anymore. Like I thought if I could show them how cool and lovely you are, they might stop being dicks, but… it didn't work
Cool and lovely??
Well you ARE
I don't expect you to dump your friends for me...
Oh they're dumped. They're all dumped. Anyone who's mean to you is officially dumped forEVER
Sai and Christian from rugby are nice! And Otis sometimes!! But yeah… I don't think any of the others like me...
TAP
TAP
TAP

To be honest I don't think I have many good friends... I don't really have any very close friends apart from you

I'm really sorry

Well I think my friends want to adopt you into our friendship group 😃

Omg

They liked me then?? Because they're all so nice and I definitely wanna hang out with them more!!

Of course they liked you Nick you are the loveliest person in the whole entire world

SSHHH don't make me flustered

TAP
TAP
TAP
BRUSH
BRUSH
TAP
TAP
TAP
TAP
TAP
TAP
TAP
TAP
TAP
TAP

TAP TAP
Hey so I needed to tell you th
something kinda bad happened
after you left tonight... me and
Harry got in a fight and
then
I
DELETE
You still ok to come over tomorrow??
Because I sorta have an idea
Do you wanna go on a proper date?
Omg... Formally asking me out.... This sounds slightly more sophisticated than just making out in our bedrooms
but yes of cOURSE

what shall we do?😃
Can I make it a surprise??
Omg okay!! I'm so excited alkjsdfldsg
Nick I like you so much
You're my favorite person
You're MY favorite person!!!!!!!!!!
Charlie??
LOL did you fall asleep
Z Z Z Z
Z Z Z
1:27

1:28
Sunday, May 23
Nick
I'm gonna fall asleep too but I just want you to know that you're the best and I'm gonna kiss you a lot tomorrow ♡

THE NEXT MORNING
Pfft- Nellie!!
LICK
You're so cute! Aren't you!!

boof?
Nellie!
BORK
BORK
Hey
PANT
PANT
Hey!

What happened?
Oh... yeah... erm...

So, I kind of got in a fight with Harry.
When you left and I got back to the group, he started saying a lot of shitty things about you. And I just lost it and... I punched him.
Oh...
Nick...

But, like, I immediately regretted it and stopped. And that's when he punched me.
I guess he managed to hit me really hard, haha
SQUEEEZE

You big idiot... why are you so great
??
Why didn't you tell me last night?
I was embarrassed...it was stupid, sinking to his level
Well, actually-

As much as I hate seeing you get hurt,
Harry really deserved a proper punch in the face
Hahaha!! You are SUCH a Slytherin!
And you're 100% Gryffindor!

How are we even dating?
Because I'm so hot, I turned a straight boy?
That may be true but TOO SOON
Ha ha ha!
Now can you tell me where we're going?
Nope! Still a surprise ☺
Platform 2

I haven't been this way before!
RUMBLE
RUMBLE
SCREE
SCREE
Come on, we're nearly there!
Haha okay okay!
SCREE
Seagulls?
SCREE
SCREE
SCREE

Oh my god
Here we are!
OUR MARIN
The beach?!!

SPLASH

Ahhh!
PADDLE
SHAKE
SIT
Oh no
Ha ha ha!

You wanna share?
Okay!
FISH & CHIPS
30
30

café
Photobooth inside
Oh my god
EN
Photobooth!
Photobooth!
You know that time we went to the arcade
and went in the photobooth?

And you made me sit on your lap?
I did not MAKE you-
I distinctly remember you literally pulling me onto your lap
Um
STAND

ah
SIT
I wanted to kiss you so bad when that happened
me too

15 MINUTES LATER...
COLLECT PHOTOS
APPEAR
FLATTEN
HA
HA
HA
HA
HA
HA

DIG
DIG

DIG
DIG
?
!

Still Together
Mac DeMarco
0:12
3:27

Yesterday...
you said you didn't want me to cover for you anymore...
Does that mean you want to come out?

...
Yeah
Yeah, it does.

you really want to??
Yeah, I- I know I've been unsure about it for a while, but-
I'm definitely bisexual.
And I don't want to have to creep around,
pretending we're just friends

I'm not saying I want to make some sort of public announcement, haha...
But I want to tell the people I care about
And I want you to be able to tell people, too.
BRUSH

Ha ha, ha!
I like you so much!!!
And I love liking you!
?
?

I LIKE CHARLIE SPRING!
...
IN A ROMANTIC WAY NOT JUST A FRIEND WAY
HA
HA
HA!

Oh... Char, what-
S-sorry
I'm just... really happy

I never thought this would happen to me
SNIFF
Oh Char...
me neither ♥

Nick?
yeah?
so...
Does this mean we're boyfriends?

...
er, yes??

Was that not established the last ten times I made out with you??
Oh- yeah- I don't know, we never talked about it??
...
HA
HA
HA
HA
HA
Why are we like this??!

LIFT
I'M YOUR BOYFRIEND!!
AAAH
YOU'RE MY BOYFRIEND!!
RUN
WE'RE BOYFRIENDS!!
Nick!! Don't drop me!!

COLLAPSE
HA
HA
HA
HA

And now we're gonna tell people

yeah...
Hey, Mum
Hi, Nicky!

You seem smiley! Did you and Charlie have a good day?
Yeah we did!
We went to the beach and just chilled out for a few hours. It was so much fun!
POUR
We went paddling and explored the town a little bit! And got fish and chips!

Sounds like a lovely day!
Yeah!
Hey, Nellie! Did you have a good day?
Boof!
...

Mum?
Mmhm?
You know Charlie's, like...
my best friend?

...
If you're going to ask if he can come to Menorca with us this summer, the answer is no, I already booked the tickets and-
No...
No, that's not what I was gonna say...

He's my boyfriend.

Charlie's my boyfriend.

I- I still like girls, but... I like guys, too, I think...
And Charlie, we're- we're going out
I wanted you to know

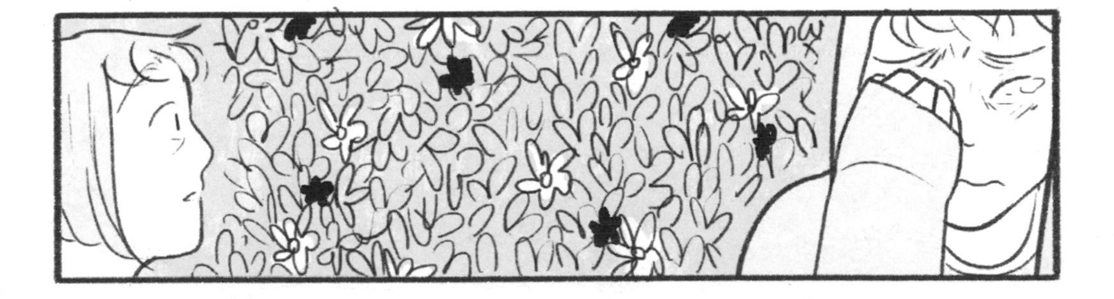

STAND
Oh,
baby...

SNIFF

Thank you for telling me
sob

Thank you for telling me that

Sshh. It's okay.
WIPE
Sweetheart, you don't have to say you like girls if you don't...
No, I- I definitely like both!!

It's- it's called... um... bisexuality... if you've heard of that
chuckle
Yes, I've heard of that. I wasn't born in 1920.

HA
HA
SNIFF

How long have you known?

Well... me and Charlie started going out, like, a month and a half ago...
but I started liking him way before that...
Months ago.

I wanted to tell you, but we never talk about, like, gay stuff.
I didn't know how you would react.
Are you surprised?
...
I... had my suspicions. Especially after seeing how much you care about him. But...
I was never sure.

...
I love you, Nicky.
I'm sorry I ever made you feel like you couldn't tell me that.

Love you, too.

And Charlie still can't come to Menorca with us, even though he's your boyfriend.
But MUUUUUM

David got to bring his girlfriend last year!!

Your brother is four years older than you and they were living together at uni at the time-

ZZz

But Muuuuum... I thought you loved meeeeee...

SIGH Nicholas...

Heartstopper will continue in
Volume 3!

CASUAL CLOTHES
Charlie is always cold and has therefore developed a love for woolly clothing, particularly woolly sweaters. Charlie likes anything snuggly and oversized. The only thing that can beat a woolly sweater is one of Nick's hoodies.
T-shirts take up most of Nick's wardrobe. He has far too many but is too attached to them to get rid of any.
Skinny jeans are a Charlie Spring wardrobe staple. They work for every occasion, right?
Nick likes comfortable and sporty clothes more than anything. He'd wear joggers every day if he could!
Nick's very much a fan of patterned socks. Especially if they have dogs on them.

SMART CLOTHES

I realized something last night.
I really really really REALLY like Charlie.
So today I went to his house and we kissed AGAIN. MULTIPLE TIMES.

I kinda meant to talk to him about last night first but he just started saying sorry over and over again because he thought I rejected him – my own fault for running off like a nervous idiot!! Add that to the fact that he looked extremely adorable in his pajamas and socks and his hair was all fluffy because he'd just woken up... and his dimples... his eyes are so fucking blue... uh... YEAH anyway, he kept looking at me like he really wanted to kiss me, so I just DID IT. And he kissed me back!!!! HE LIKES ME BACK!!!

I think I gave him a bit of a shock, tbh. Like, he didn't realize I liked him until that moment. Gonna have to kiss him MANY more times, just to get my point across. :)

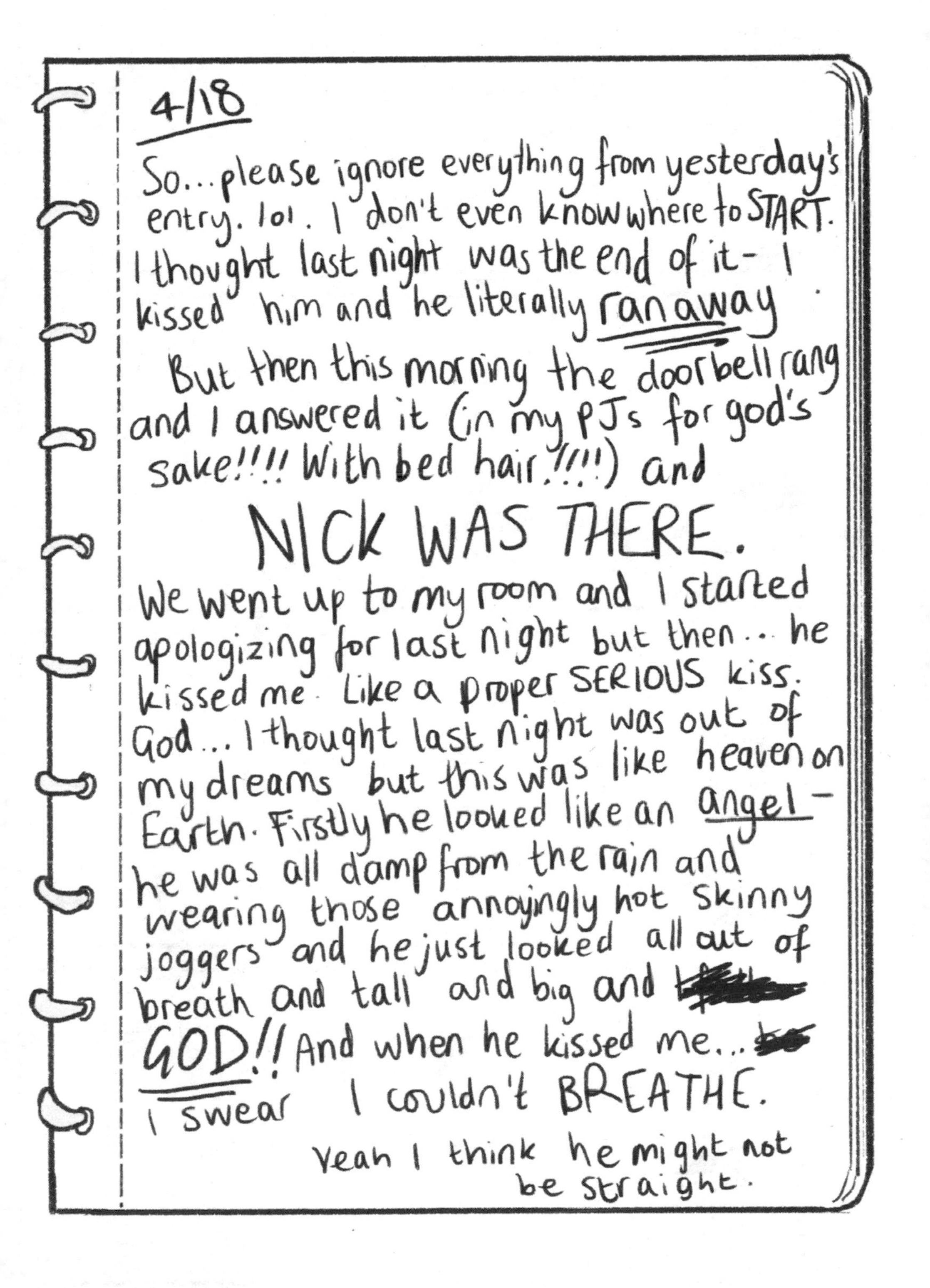
4/18
So... please ignore everything from yesterday's
entry. lol. I don't even know where to START.
I thought last night was the end of it - I
kissed him and he literally ran away.
But then this morning the doorbell rang
and I answered it (in my PJs for god's
sake!!!! With bed hair!!!!) and
NICK WAS THERE.
We went up to my room and I started
apologizing for last night but then... he
kissed me. Like a proper SERIOUS kiss.
God... I thought last night was out of
my dreams but this was like heaven on
Earth. Firstly he looked like an angel -
he was all damp from the rain and
wearing those annoyingly hot skinny
joggers and he just looked all out of
breath and tall and big and
GOD!! And when he kissed me...
I swear I couldn't BREATHE.
Yeah I think he might not
be straight.

NAME: CHARLES "CHARLIE" SPRING
WHO ARE YOU: NICK'S BOYFRIEND
SCHOOL YEAR: YEAR 10 **AGE:** 15
BIRTHDAY: APRIL 27TH

NAME: Nicholas "Nick" Nelson
WHO ARE YOU: Charlie's boyfriend
SCHOOL YEAR: Year 11 **AGE:** 16
BIRTHDAY: September 4th

NAME: Tao Xu
WHO ARE YOU: Charlie's friend
SCHOOL YEAR: Year 10 **AGE:** 15
BIRTHDAY: September 23rd

NAME: VICTORIA "TORI" SPRING
WHO ARE YOU: CHARLIE'S SISTER
SCHOOL YEAR: YEAR 11 **AGE:** 16
BIRTHDAY: APRIL 5TH

NAME: Tara Jones

WHO ARE YOU: Nick's friend

SCHOOL YEAR: Year 11 **AGE:** 15

BIRTHDAY: July 3rd

NAME: HARRY GREENE

WHO ARE YOU: NICK'S CLASSMATE

SCHOOL YEAR: YEAR 11 **AGE:** 16

BIRTHDAY: APRIL 17TH

NAME: Elle Argent

WHO ARE YOU: Charlie's friend

NAME: Aled Last

WHO ARE YOU: Charlie's friend

NAME: Darcy Olsson

WHO ARE YOU: Tara's girlfriend

The Practice Room
A HEARTSTOPPER MINI-COMIC
PRACTICE ROOM B
HIGGS MUSIC NIGHT
TONIGHT
7:00
MANY MONTHS AGO....
6:46
Reminder: School Concert 14 mins
Jonesy! Hey!
Darcy!! Why are you here? I'm practicing!!
The concert starts soon!!

I joined the orchestra, didn't I? I'm here to practice, same as you!
DOOR STOP
THE DOOR!!
IT'S BROKEN! IT LOCKS BY ITSELF!
Huh?
CLICK
We're locked in.

5 MINS LATER
No signal??
10 MINS LATER
HELP
20 MINS LATER
Someone will come soon
IGNORE
Hey... I'm really sorry... We might get out in time for the second half!
HUFF
Are you ignoring me?
Yes!
Haha, I made you speak!
UGH!
Jonesy... seriously, what is your problem with me?

You're just so...
ANNOYING
You're loud and you're always making STUPID jokes and you can't even play the trumpet properly
and you STOLE MY FAVORITE PEN.
... pen?
Ah! Yeah, I brought it tonight to give it back
You let me borrow it in French and I totally forgot!
Here
...thanks

half an hour later...
SILENCE
Ha, you really hate me, don't you.
I don't HATE you.
JAZZ
Opera
But you find me annoying?
No... I didn't mean that. You're just hard not to notice.
Uh... I mean...

I...
I'm just sick of being stuck in here. I want to go home.
Oh... Tara...
It's okay
Someone will come soon

Blues
Your mascara has smeared all over your eyes. Just so you know.
Shut up!!
Where?
Hana tricked you!
I have a pen!! I WILL draw on you!!
AHH

DON'T YOU DARE
REVENGE
PIN
AAA
okay... just do it

PULL

!!
Tara? Darcy? Are you down here??
Miss!! We're locked in here!!
DAZED
Goodness! I'm glad I found you in time for the second half!
Thanks, miss
LEAVE
What... just happened...
The end...?

Author's Note

I'm amazed, overjoyed, and so grateful that there are now two whole volumes of Heartstopper. How on Earth have I managed to fill up that many pieces of paper? I'm so happy and excited to be telling this story and I very much hope you've been enjoying it so far.

Heartstopper focused largely on Nick and his coming-out journey in this volume. I aimed to write the sort of story I would have loved to see when I was a teenager. Everyone deserves the time, space, and support to figure out their feelings and their identity. But even if you don't have a supportive partner, like Charlie, or a loving parent, like Nick's mum, or even just an adorable dog like Nellie to cuddle when things get tough, I promise that one day you will find someone who loves you just the way you are.

My biggest thanks is to all the online readers of Heartstopper, my Patreon patrons, and the Kickstarter supporters. Your support for the comic is the reason you're holding this book in your hands!

To Rachel Wade and the whole team at Hachette: I'm so thankful for the love you've shown my little comic and I feel so lucky to have found such a passionate group of people.

Thanks to my incredible agent, Claire Wilson, without whom I would probably be a mess.

And thank you, dear reader, for tuning in to Nick and Charlie's story once again.

I can't wait to tell you more in the next volume.

Alice

x

Alice Oseman was born in 1994 in Kent, England, and is a full-time writer and illustrator. She can usually be found staring aimlessly at computer screens, questioning the meaninglessness of existence, or doing anything and everything to avoid getting an office job.

As well as writing and illustrating Heartstopper, Alice is the author of three YA novels: *Solitaire*, *Radio Silence*, and *I Was Born for This*.

To find out more about Alices work, visit her online:

aliceoseman.com
twitter.com/AliceOseman
instagram.com/aliceoseman

Nick!!
I can
walk!
This is
faster!